Dial Books for Young Readers
An imprint of Penguin Random House LLC, New York

Visit us online at penguinrandomhouse.com

Printed in China • ISBN 9780525553816
Design by Lily Malcom • Text set in Egyptian Slate Pro
Special Markets ISBN: 9780593111772 Not for resale
10 9 8 7 6 5 4 3 2

This Imagination Library edition is published by Penguin Young Readers, a division
of Penguin Random House, exclusively for Dolly Parton's Imagination Library,
a not-for-profit program designed to inspire a love of reading and learning, sponsored
in part by The Dollywood Foundation. Penguin's trade editions of this work are
available wherever books are sold.

This bilingual edition provides a rhyming adaptation in Spanish of the original English text.

For extra fun, look at the travel patches
on the endpapers. Can you match the
picture in each patch to its related
image in the story?

Para mayor diversión, observa los botones
de viaje al inicio y final del libro. ¿Puedes
relacionar la imagen de cada botón con su
imagen en el cuento?

For Trixie and Max, with love
—J.G.

A Trixie y Max, con amor
—J.G.

To my friend Irene, a traveler mouse
—B.G.

A mi amiga Irene, ratoncita viajera
—B.G.

Red House
Tree House
Little Bitty Brown Mouse

by Jane Godwin ✳ illustrated by Blanca Gómez

Casa del árbol
Casa rojita
Diminuta Ratoncita Marroncita

Jane Godwin ✳ ilustrado por Blanca Gómez

Versión rimada en español por Yanitzia Canetti

Dial Books for Young Readers

Red house

    Blue house

Green house

    Tree house!

See the tiny mouse

in her little brown house?

Casa roja

    Casa azul

Casa verde

    y en el árbol, ¡una casita!

¿Ves en su casa marrón

a una linda ratoncita?

Blue flower

Pink flower

Purple flower

Red.

Can you count the petals

in the garden bed?

Flor azul
Flor rosada
Flor roja
y morada.

¿Puedes contar los pétalos
de estas flores perfumadas?

White rabbit
Gray rabbit
Black rabbit
Brown.

Floppy rabbit ears
going up and going down.

Conejo blanco
Conejo gris
Conejo negro
y marrón.

Orejas flexibles de conejo
yendo en cualquier dirección.

Yellow fruit   Do you know the color

    Pink fruit   of the berries in between?

Orange fruit

    Green.

Fruta amarilla

Fruta rosada

Fruta verde

y anaranjada.

¿Sabes de qué color son
las bayas amontonadas?

Pink shoes

    Blue shoes

Green shoes

    Red.

Shoes go on your feet.

What goes on your head?

Zapatos azules
   Zapatos rosados
Zapatos verdes
   y colorados.

Los zapatos en tus pies.
¿Y en tu cabeza qué ves?

Purple fish
Orange fish—
rainbow
tail.

Tiny darting silver fish . . .
one gigantic whale!

Pez morado

Pez naranja:

cola arcoíris

brillante.

Veloz pececillo plateado . . .

¡y una ballena gigante!

Ice cream
   that's smooth
And ice cream
   that's spotted.

Would you like the white one
or the one that's dotted?

Helado
   cremoso
y helado
   con pintitas.

¿Prefieres el blanco
o el que tiene chispitas?

Red boat
    Yellow boat
Green boat
    Pink.

Uh-oh . . .
Don't let that boat sink!

Barco rojo
Barco amarillo
Barco verde
y rosado.

¡Ay! ¡Que no se hunda!
¿Qué ha pasado?

Orange bird
    Green bird
Gray bird's
    feather.

Watch the birds now,
flying all together.

Pájaro naranja
    Pájaro verde
De plumas grises,
    un pajarito.

¡Mira cómo vuelan
todos juntitos!

Purple bike

Red bike

Scooter zooming

past.

Ding Ding   Beep Beep   W h e e !   That's fast!

Bicicleta morada

Bicicleta roja

Motocicleta que pasa

velozmente.

Ring Ring   Piii Piii   ¡Y u p i !   ¡Rápidamente!

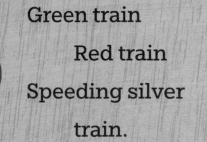

Green train
Red train
Speeding silver
train.

See the trains sparkle
in the sun and in the rain?

Tren verde
Tren rojo
Plateado y veloz
va un tren.

Bajo la luna y el sol,
¡qué brillantes se ven!

Brown dog
Red dog
Dog with a
spot.

Dogs that are friendly,
and dogs that are not.

DOGTEL

HOTEL

Perro con una
   manchita
Perro rojo
   Perro marrón.

Perros que son amigables
y perros que no lo son.

One, two,
three balloons
gently floating
by.

Drifting in the breeze,
and up into the sky.

Uno, dos,
tres globos
que flotan
suavemente

Flotan en la brisa
hacia el cielo libremente.

Yellow sun
Silver rain
Clouds white and
gray.

See the rainbow colors
on a sunny rainy day?

Nubes blancas

y grises

Sol amarillo

Lluvia plateada.

¿Ves los colores del arcoíris

en la mañana lluviosa y soleada?

Colors on a
sunny street—
what's your favorite
house?

fish market

Is it red or blue or green . . .

Colores en una
calle soleada:
¿cuál es tu casa
favorita?

¿La roja, la azul o la verdecita...?

and did you spot that mouse?

¿Encontraste a la ratoncita?

ICE CREAM

Doug

TRAIN
10